THUDD

Hiya! My name Thudd. Best robot friend of Drewd. Thudd know lotsa stuff about deserts. What bug is good to eat. How to get drink from frog. How spiders live underground.

Drewd like to invent stuff. Thudd help! But Drewd make lotsa mistakes. Drewd invent shrinking machine. Now Drewd small as ant. Unkie Al try to help Drewd get big again. But gotta go through desert first. Hot! Hot! Hot! Lotsa danger, too. Thudd worried. Want to see what happen? Turn page, please!

Get lost with
Andrew, Judy, and Thudd
in all their exciting adventures!

*Andrew Lost on the Dog*
*Andrew Lost in the Bathroom*
*Andrew Lost in the Kitchen*
*Andrew Lost in the Garden*
*Andrew Lost Under Water*
*Andrew Lost in the Whale*
*Andrew Lost on the Reef*
*Andrew Lost in the Deep*
*Andrew Lost in Time*
*Andrew Lost on Earth*
*Andrew Lost with the Dinosaurs*
*Andrew Lost in the Ice Age*
*Andrew Lost in the Garbage*
*Andrew Lost with the Bats*
*Andrew Lost in the Jungle*
*Andrew Lost in Uncle Al*
*Andrew Lost in the Desert*

AND COMING SOON!
*Andrew Lost with the Frogs*

# ANDREW LOST

## BY J. C. GREENBURG

## ILLUSTRATED
## BY JAN GERARDI

**17**

**IN THE DESERT**

A STEPPING STONE BOOK™

Random House 🏠 New York

*To Dan, Zack, and the real Andrew,*
*with a galaxy of love.*
*To the children who read these books: I wish*
*you wonderful questions. Questions are*
*telescopes into the universe!*
*—J.C.G.*

*To Cathy Goldsmith, with many thanks.*
*—J.G.*

Text copyright © 2008 by J. C. Greenburg
Illustrations copyright © 2008 by Jan Gerardi

All rights reserved. Published in the United States by Random House Children's Books, a division of Random House, Inc., New York.

Random House and colophon are registered trademarks and A Stepping Stone Book and colophon are trademarks of Random House, Inc. Andrew Lost is a trademark of J. C. Greenburg.

Visit us on the Web!
www.randomhouse.com/kids/AndrewLost
www.AndrewLost.com

Educators and librarians, for a variety of teaching tools, visit us at www.randomhouse.com/teachers

*Library of Congress Cataloging-in-Publication Data*
Greenburg, J. C. (Judith C.)
In the desert / by J. C. Greenburg ; illustrated by Jan Gerardi. — 1st ed.
    p.    cm. — (Andrew Lost ; 17) "A Stepping Stone Book."
Summary: While in the Australian desert, ant-sized Andrew, his cousin Judy, and Thudd the robot are carried away by a dust devil and face many dangerous creatures, from a flock of wild parakeets to a Perentie lizard, as they try to make their way back to Uncle Al.
ISBN 978-0-375-84667-0 (trade) — ISBN 978-0-375-94667-7 (lib. bdg.)
[1. Deserts—Fiction. 2. Desert animals—Fiction. 3. Robots—Fiction.
4. Cousins—Fiction. 5. Australia—Fiction.] I. Gerardi, Jan, ill.
II. Title. III. Series.
PZ7.G82785Ink 2008      [Fic]—dc22        2007012802

Printed in the United States of America
10 9 8 7 6 5 4 3 2 1   First Edition

# CONTENTS

# ANDREW'S WORLD

### Andrew Dubble

Andrew is ten years old, but he's been inventing things since he was four. His inventions usually get him in trouble, like the time he accidentally took the Time-A-Tron on a trip to the beginning of the universe.

Andrew's newest invention was supposed to save the world from getting buried in garbage. Instead, it squashed Andrew and his cousin Judy down to beetle size. They got hauled off to a dump, thrown up by a sea-gull, and carried off to the Australian rain forest on the back of a bird. Now they're crossing the Australian desert with their uncle Al to see if his partner can help them get un-shrunk. But a lot of dangerous surprises lurk in the desert. And Andrew and Judy are about to meet up with them.

### Judy Dubble

Judy is Andrew's thirteen-year-old cousin. She's been snuffled into a dog's nose, was pooped out of a whale, and had her pajamas chewed by a Tyrannosaurus—all because of Andrew. Judy had been hoping that her life would get back to normal. Unfortunately, that's not going to happen today.

### Thudd

**T**he **H**andy **U**ltra-**D**igital **D**etective. Thudd is a super-smart robot and Andrew's best friend. He has helped save Andrew and Judy from the exploding sun, the giant squid, and the really weird stuff inside Uncle Al. Now can he protect his buddies from the deadly desert?

## The Goa Constrictor

This giant fake snake is Andrew's newest invention. *Goa* is sort of short for **Ga**rbage **Go**es **A**way. The Goa is supposed to keep the world from getting buried in garbage by squashing rotting vegetables, green meat, and dirty diapers down to teensy-weensy specks. Unfortunately for Andrew and Judy, the Goa doesn't just shrink garbage. In two minutes and one stinky burp, the Goa can shrink anything—and anyone!

At first the Goa shrank Andrew and Judy to the size of beetles. But since then, they've been changing size more often than some people change their underwear!

# HOT! HOT! HOT!

"Erf!" said ant-sized Andrew Dubble. He was inside an empty bottle cap, bouncing into his cousin Judy.

Their uncle Al had glued the bottle cap to the dashboard of his jeep. It made a safe perch for Andrew and Judy to see the Australian desert as Uncle Al drove through it. Uncle Al had even made them tiny sunglasses from a strip of dark plastic.

"Get off of me, Bug-Brain," said Judy, shoving Andrew away. "It's *soooo* hot in here!"

"Urp!" Andrew burped a big garlicky burp. *That pizza crumb sure tasted good,* he thought.

"Disgusting boy!" said Judy.

Uncle Al turned his eyes from the black ribbon of road and glanced in their direction. He adjusted the leaf he had arranged above their heads like a bug-sized umbrella to shade them from the sun.

"It's a rough trip through the desert, guys," said Uncle Al. "The air conditioner isn't working, so you'd better settle in for a long, hot, bumpy ride."

*meep* . . . "Desert air hot, hot, hot!" came a squeaky voice from Andrew's shirt pocket. "Desert sand even hotter. Can fry egg on desert sand."

It was Andrew's little silver robot friend, Thudd. Uncle Al had invented him.

"I'm getting hungry again," said Andrew.

Uncle Al smiled and mopped his face with a handkerchief. "Well, we won't be stopping for sandy fried eggs," he said. "It's almost three o'clock. We're supposed to meet up with my partner, Winka, by eight p.m. She's taking pictures of meteor showers deep in the desert. Winka has an idea about how to get you guys unshrunk."

Andrew's latest invention, the Goa Constrictor, was supposed to shrink garbage. But the first time Andrew tried it, he ended up shrinking himself, and Judy and Thudd, too.

Andrew nodded. "Winka helped us escape from the dinosaurs sixty-five million years ago," he said. "I'll bet she can help us now."

"Before we get stepped on or swatted," said Judy.

The afternoon sun burned through the windshield. *This must be what it feels like to get cooked,* thought Andrew.

The yellow sand stretched on forever. Here and there, patches of tall, prickly grass looked like sleeping herds of spiny porcupines. Sometimes a scraggly tree poked up like a skeleton. Now and then, a tumbleweed rolled across the road. There wasn't a house or a sign of another human being anywhere.

"The desert is like an empty planet," said Andrew.

Uncle Al shook his head. "It looks that way now," he said. "But the desert is full of life. Lots of strange creatures are resting or hiding underground during the hottest hours. They'll come out to hunt when the sun goes down.

"The plants look pretty scraggly. But when rain comes, the desert looks like a flower garden. Some seeds and plants come to life almost instantly with just a little water."

"Humph," said Judy. "I haven't even seen a cactus."

Uncle Al nodded. "There are no native cactuses in the Australian desert," he said.

*Oinga! Oinga! Oinga!* came a sound from the front of the jeep. The jeep was slowing down.

*Plunk . . . plunk . . . erk . . .*

The jeep rolled to a stop. A ribbon of steam was curling from under the hood.

Uncle Al shook his head. "I'll find out what's wrong," he said. "And while I'm doing that, I want you guys to stay put. The desert is a dangerous place. Some of the most deadly animals in the world live here. And not all of them sleep during the day."

"Okey-dokey, Unkie!" squeaked Thudd.

Uncle Al got out of the jeep and opened the hood. A cloud of steam puffed out.

"We've got a leak," yelled Uncle Al from the front of the car. "I need to check underneath the jeep. This may take a while."

The heat was making Andrew sleepy. He rested his head against the edge of the bottle cap.

Out of the corner of his eye, Andrew caught a glimpse of something moving. He turned to see a dark cloud whirling near the ground. It was spinning like a top and whipping up the sand. It was heading straight toward the jeep!

# 2 WILLY-NILLY

Andrew climbed out of the bottle cap and onto the dashboard.

"Get back here, Bug-Brain!" yelled Judy. "Uncle Al told us to stay put!"

"Wowzers schnauzers!" hollered Andrew. "There's a tornado out there! Uncle Al is under the jeep. I'll bet he doesn't even see it!"

"Cheese Louise!" said Judy.

*meep* . . . "Called dust devil," squeaked Thudd. "Australian people call it willy-willy.

"Air near sand get super-hot. Super-hot air light, light, light! Little shove from breeze make air spin. Spinning air pick up sand. Make willy-willy."

"Stuff a sock in it, Thudd!" said Judy. "The windows are wide open! We'll get blown away!"

*meep* . . . "Time for purple-button message!" squeaked Thudd.

There were three rows of three buttons on Thudd's chest. All the buttons glowed green except for a big purple one in the middle. This was the button for sending an emergency message to Uncle Al's Hologram Helper.

Thudd pressed the purple button. It blinked three times and went off.

Andrew glanced around. Nothing on the dashboard could protect them from the powerful wind.

Then he looked toward the window. He grabbed Judy's arm. "Come on," he said, pulling her toward the opening.

"Are you nuts-o?" said Judy, pulling away.

"Hurry!" yelled Andrew. "We can hide in the space where the window goes down!"

They rushed toward the window on the driver's side.

*Whewwwwwwwwwww* . . . came the windy sound of the willy-willy from the passenger's side.

They were an inch away from the window when the hot gust hit them. Andrew felt that a giant hair dryer was blowing burning sand against his skin. He closed his eyes to keep out the stinging grains. A sneeze tickled the back of his nose.

*Whoooooooooosh!*

Andrew felt his feet lift off the dashboard. He was blowing away like a candy wrapper in a hurricane!

*"Aaaaaaaaah!"* came Judy's voice through the sound of the wind. Judy was squeezing his arm like a boa constrictor.

Andrew's stomach jumped and sank as the wind hurled them up and dragged them down and spun them round and round.

*WHOOOOOOOOOOOOSH!*

The wind drowned Judy's screams.

*Where will the willy-willy take us?* Andrew wondered. *How will Uncle Al ever find us in this humongous desert?*

Spinning and spinning, Andrew got too dizzy to think about anything but feeling sick. *"URP!"* A giant garlic burp exploded from his stomach.

Just as it seemed the willy-willy would drag them through the desert forever, the twisting wind began to slow. Andrew felt himself dropping.

"Yeeeouch!" His butt had slammed into something hard. And he was underwater! His feet couldn't touch the bottom and there was water up his nose! He held his breath and popped to the surface.

"Blaaargh!" Judy spluttered.

"Holy moly!" said Andrew, opening his eyes. As he treaded water, Andrew saw they had landed in a big, warm puddle beneath a scrawny bush. Judy was bobbing next to him.

Thudd had pulled himself up out of Andrew's pocket, crept up his shirt, and climbed on top of his head.

"It rained in *this* part of the desert! A *lot!*" said Andrew.

*"Yoop! Yoop! Yoop!"* said Thudd. "Like Unkie said. Maybe not get lotsa rain for lotsa years. When rain come, water collect in holes. Stay for little while."

"Better drink while we can," said Andrew. He dipped his head and began to slurp.

"Yikes!" yelped Judy. She splashed madly toward the edge of the puddle. "Something bit my foot!"

*meep* . . . "Dinosaur shrimp!" said Thudd. "Little shrimp hatch from tiny eggs when rain come. Grow fast. Lay eggs in few days.

"When puddle dry up, shrimp die. But eggs can live lotsa years till rains come. Then eggs hatch."

Andrew dog-paddled quickly after Judy.

They reached the puddle's shore and climbed onto the shady sand beneath the bush.

Andrew took in the landscape. Clumps of spiky grass were like islands of giant needles in an ocean of sand. Stony mounds rose high above the grass.

*They look as big as skyscrapers to me,* thought Andrew. *But they're probably as tall as Uncle Al.*

Far away, a huge wall of rock glowed orange in the sun.

But there was no jeep, no Uncle Al. This wasn't the part of the desert they had been driving through.

"Where *are* we?" asked Judy.

Andrew shrugged his shoulders. "Maybe Uncle Al will know when he calls us back. There's a little shade under this bush and we've got the puddle for water. We can wait here till Uncle Al comes to get us."

*Cheweeet! Chweet! Ch . . . ch . . . ch . . . Chaweeet!*

A flock of brightly colored birds, blue ones and green ones, swooped overhead.

"Parakeets!" said Judy.

*meep* . . . "Lotsa birds in desert," said Thudd. "Lotsa bugs for birds to eat."

"I don't see any bugs," said Andrew.

Judy tucked herself close to the stem of the bush. "*We're* bug-sized, Bug-Brain!"

*meep* . . . "Some bugs got colors that hide them," said Thudd. "Called camouflage. Other bugs just hide."

"KAA-muh-flahj" flashed across his face screen.

"Look!" said Thudd. He pointed to a dark bump in the shady sand under a twig.

Andrew crept over to see. The bump had two wiry antennas sticking out of it—and two round black eyes!

"Aw," said Andrew. "A dead bug."

"Noop! Noop! Noop!" said Thudd. "Live cricket. Bury itself in sand to hide, to keep cool. Sand cool underneath."

Suddenly something snapped around Andrew's chest from behind. "YEEEEOUCH!" he hollered as sharp spines dug into his ribs.

Andrew's feet made a tiny trail in the sand. Then something dragged him up into the bush.

# YOU'D HAVE TO BE AWFULLY THIRSTY TO DRINK THAT

*"Androoooo!"* hollered Judy. She grabbed on to Andrew's feet and pulled.

Andrew looked up at a pair of huge, toothy pliers—open wide! "Bug jaws!" hollered Andrew.

*meep* . . . "Katydid!" said Thudd. "Kinda big grasshopper. Eat leaves. Eat bugs!

"Katydid got good camouflage. Hide in bush. Look like twig. Wait for prey."

"It could bite my head off with one chomp!" said Andrew. His heart was beating like a bongo drum. Frantically, he tried to pry the katydid's stiff legs off of his chest.

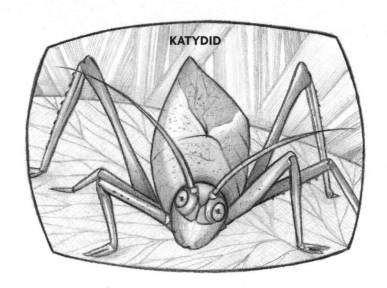

KATYDID

The katydid was dragging him up into the bush.

*meep* . . . "Katydid hide from birds," said Thudd.

*Plump . . . Plop . . . Ploop . . .*

The sound was coming from the puddle. Andrew craned his neck to look. The puddle was bubbling!

Two big black eyes the size of marbles popped out of the puddle. They stared unblinkingly in Andrew's direction. The creature slowly crept toward the edge of the puddle. Its body looked like a round, puffy brown cushion.

*Mwaaah . . . mwaaah . . . mwaaah . . . meep . . .* "Water-holding frog!" squeaked Thudd. "Drink lotsa water when rain come to desert. Then dig tunnel underground. Make cocoon out of old skin. Can stay underground for five years! Come up when rain come again.

"Sometime thirsty humans dig up water-holding frog. Stick frog butt in mouth and squeeze. Out come water."

"Yuck! Yuck! Yuck!" gagged Judy, dangling from Andrew's feet. "I wouldn't drink water from a frog butt if I was dying of thirst!"

"Frogs eat bugs," said Andrew as the katydid dragged him higher up the bush—and closer to its jaws. "And that frog must be really hungry if it's been underground for five years."

"You're going to get eaten by a stupid bug!" hollered Judy. "And I'm going to get eaten by a dumb frog! This is all your fault, Bug-Brain!"

*meep* . . . "Got idea!" squeaked Thudd. "Remember when Drewd fight off beetle in bat cave? Katydids and crickets not like garlic. Drewd got garlic breath. Gotta blow garlic breath on katydid knees."

"On its *knees*?" said Judy.

*meep* . . . "Katydid smell with knees," said Thudd.

"Blow on them?" said Andrew. "I can do better than that!"

Andrew leaned close to one of the prickly legs that had him in its grip.

"URRRRRP!" Up came a giant burp of garlic breath.

Suddenly the insect pulled its sharp spines out of Andrew's ribs. He and Judy were falling!

*Splop!*

Andrew and Judy splashed down into a smaller puddle.

*Splat!*

The fat frog jumped out of the mud

toward the bush. In one flick of the frog's
tongue, the katydid disappeared.

*Mwaaah . . . mwaaah . . . mwaaah . . .*

The frog hopped into a nearby patch of

grass. He stopped to munch, then disappeared behind a pile of stones.

"Woofers!" said Andrew, scooping mud off his pants. "Let's look for a safer place to stay."

Just then, the purple button in the middle of Thudd's chest began to blink.

It popped open and a beam of purple light zoomed out. At the end of the beam was a pale purple hologram of Uncle Al.

"Hi, Uncle Al!" shouted Andrew.

"Hiya, Unkie!" squeaked Thudd.

"Where are you, Uncle Al?" hollered Judy.

"What's important is where are *you*?" said Uncle Al.

When Uncle Al visited Andrew and Judy by using his Hologram Helper, he could hear them but not see them.

"I don't know," said Judy, "but we almost got eaten by a katydid. Then we almost got eaten by a frog."

Uncle Al's fuzzy eyebrows met in the middle of his forehead. "Good golly, Miss Molly!" he exclaimed. "I'd better find you before you almost get eaten by something else! Are you near anything big?"

"We can see a giant wall of rock," said Andrew. "But it's awfully far away."

"That must be Uluru," said Uncle Al. "It's the highest spot in this desert.

"It's such a beautiful place that people come to see it. There are hotels and restaurants. We can meet there."

"But how can we *get* there?" asked Judy. "It's far away and we're the size of *ants*!"

Uncle Al scratched his chin. "It's a problem," he said. "But solving problems is what we Dubbles do best."

Andrew nodded. "We got back from the beginning of the universe," he said. "We can figure out how to get to a rock in the desert."

"It's a windy day," said Uncle Al. "Maybe you can use the wind to . . ."

The Uncle Al hologram began to flicker like a candle flame. It crackled, popped, and disappeared.

"Uncle Al!" yelled Judy. "Come back!"

# WHAT LOOKS LIKE A WORM AND TASTES LIKE PEANUT BUTTER?

Andrew shook his head. "The Hologram Helper is probably having battery problems again," he said.

Judy checked the bush's branches for katydids before moving into the shade.

"I know how to windsurf," said Judy. "If we had something to use as a sail, we could windsurf over the sand."

"Or if we had something to make a big kite with," said Andrew. "Let's think while we walk toward Uluru."

"Humph," grumped Judy. "At our size, it could take us *months* to walk there, Bug-Brain."

"It'll take even longer if we don't start," said Andrew. "Let's go."

Andrew crept over the bush's woody roots. Suddenly he tripped and fell into a crack. He landed facedown on something soft and squishy—and wriggling.

"Holy moly!" cried Andrew. He was on top of a fat, white wormy thing squirming inside the root!

Judy peered into the cracked root as Andrew struggled out of it. *"Aaaack!"* she hollered. "There's something *disgusting* in there!"

*meep* . . . "Called witchetty grub," said Thudd. "Larva baby of big moth. Native people eat larva. Sometimes raw. Taste like egg. Sometimes cooked. Taste like peanut butter.

"This bush called witchetty bush cuz witchetty grub live in roots."

Judy rolled her eyes. "Yuck-a-rama!" she exclaimed. "Eating worms! Drinking frog water. What's *wrong* with these people?"

*meep* . . . "Australian people smart, smart, smart!" said Thudd. "Witchetty grubs and frog water lots more healthy than hot dogs and soda!"

"Urp!" burped Andrew. "I'm getting hungry. Uncle Al said there were restaurants at Uluru. Chop-chop, Judy! Let's go!"

They began plodding away from the puddle and onto the dry sand. Even with their sunglasses, the blazing sun was blinding. Andrew propped his hand over his eyes like a visor.

With the heat and the wind, their wet, muddy clothes dried quickly. Soon they were meltingly hot again. Sweat trickled down their foreheads and dripped into their eyes. But they kept on trudging toward Uluru.

After what seemed like hours, they came to a place where the tall grass didn't block their view of the distance.

"Look!" hollered Judy. "There's a patch of blue ahead! It's a lake! We can tell Uncle Al to meet us there!"

"Noop! Noop! Noop!" said Thudd. "Oody not see lake. Oody see mirage!

"In the desert, air near the ground superhot. High up, air is cool, air is heavy.

"Light travel, light bounce. When light from ground hit cool air up high, it bounce back down to ground.

"What look like blue lake is reflection of blue sky."

"Darn!" said Judy. "It's not real!"

*meep* . . . "Can take picture of mirage," said

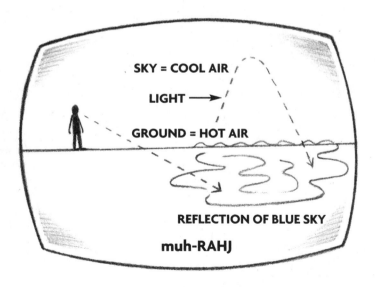

SKY = COOL AIR

LIGHT ⟶

GROUND = HOT AIR

REFLECTION OF BLUE SKY

muh-RAHJ

Thudd. "Stuff is real. Just not in place Oody see it. Like stuff in mirror."

"Neato mosquito!" said Andrew.

"Stupid, stupid mirage," complained Judy.

They were coming close to one of the mysterious tall mounds that loomed above the grass.

"Looks like a weird sand castle ahead," said Andrew.

*meep* . . . "Castle for termites," said Thudd. "Home of termite colony. Termites mix spit with dirt. Make stuff hard as cement to build mound. A million termites in colony, maybe.

"Got all kindsa rooms inside. Garden rooms. Nursery rooms for babies. Rooms for queen termite.

"Termites even got way to make breeze come through. Keep rooms cool!"

Judy frowned. "I thought termites were supposed to eat wood," she said. "There's hardly any wood in this stupid desert. Just a few scrawny trees and bushes."

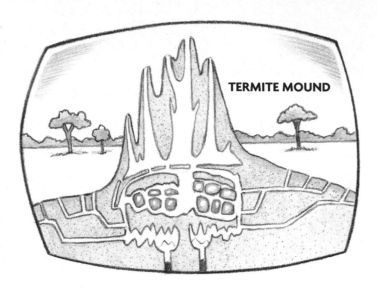

TERMITE MOUND

*meep* . . . "Desert termites eat poop and dead plants," said Thudd.

"Yuck-a-roony!" said Judy.

As they came closer to the termite mound, they saw dark streams spilling away from it. These weren't streams of water, they were rivers of insects—thousands of ants!

*meep* . . . "Meat ants!" said Thudd. "Eat up any dead animal. Even dead cow."

One of the ant streams was heading toward Andrew and Judy. The ants skittered on their skinny, stick-like legs.

Some ants were carrying plump, white wormy things in their jaws. Others dragged ant-like insects as big as themselves.

*meep* . . . "Meat ants eat live stuff, too," said Thudd. "Raiding termite colony now. Steal termite babies to eat. Take big termites, too."

"Don't move," said Andrew. "Maybe they won't notice we're here."

But ants swarmed around them. An antenna poked into Andrew's ear. Antennas were stroking Judy's hair.

*meep* . . . "Ants not got noses," Thudd said softly. "Smell stuff with antennas."

Andrew's knees were shaking. "I hope we don't smell tasty," he said.

Next to Andrew, a pair of ant jaws opened like scissors with jagged edges.

Andrew tried to back away, but ants were all around him. There was no way to escape them. The ant lunged toward Andrew. Its jaws clamped tight on his shoulder.

*"Arrrrgh!"* hollered Andrew. The ant lifted him off the ground.

*meep* . . . "Ant can carry something that weigh fifty times as much as ant!" said Thudd.

"OH *NOOOOOOO!*" hollered Judy. An ant had snapped its jaws around her middle. She pulled its antennas, but that didn't stop the ant from carrying her off.

*Holy moly!* thought Andrew. *We've been flushed down a toilet. We've been pooped out of a whale. We've almost been eaten by a Tyrannosaurus rex. But we're finally gonna end up as ant snacks!*

# TAIL ON THE LOOSE

Suddenly more ants were charging from the opposite direction. These ants were huge. Their long jaws were like jagged saws.

*meep* . . . "Bulldog ants!" said Thudd. "Fierce fighting ants! Hang on to prey and not let go!"

Some of the meat ants let go of their captured prey as they battled.

A bulldog ant lunged toward the meat ant that had captured Andrew. Both ants reared up.

Andrew looked into the round black eyes of the bulldog ant. Each eye was made up of hundreds of tiny tiles.

The antennas of the two ants touched. Their front legs tangled. The bulldog ant wrestled the meat ant to the ground.

"Burp, Drewd, *burp*!" squeaked Thudd. "Ants not like garlic smell!"

Andrew reached up and grabbed one of the ant's wiry antennas. He dragged it close to his mouth. "URRRP!" he burped loudly. *"URRRP!"*

The antenna waggled. The next instant, the ant's jaws loosened. Andrew was free! He fell to the ground and rolled clear of the battle.

Through the tangle of ant legs, he saw the meat ant that had captured Judy. It was battling another bulldog ant. They seemed to be fighting over which one would get to eat Judy. The bulldog ant clamped its jaws on Judy's neck.

Andrew crept between the two ants. *"URRRRP!"* He burped his biggest burp.

Nothing happened.

"Judy!" yelled Andrew. "Burp on your ant! You ate garlic pizza, too!"

"I don't burp, Bug-Brain!" hollered Judy.

"You can *do* it!" Andrew hollered back.

"ooo OOO OOOO *OOOOORP!*" burped Judy.

The ants' antennas waggled. Judy fell from the meat ant's jaws. The bulldog ant reared back.

Andrew and Judy tried to scramble away, but ants were everywhere. Ants were climbing on top of ants. Ants were climbing over Andrew and Judy. They could barely move.

Suddenly ants began to scatter in every direction.

To keep from being trampled, Andrew and Judy crept around a pile of rocks and onto an island of prickly grass. Andrew climbed up a stiff grass stem to see what was happening. The stem was as rough as sandpaper.

Streams of stampeding ants were flowing away from a lump in the sand. Andrew squinted to see it better.

The sand-colored lump was as big as a person's hand. Every part of its body was covered with sharp, thick white thorns. Thorns surrounded its eyes. Thorns ran up and down its neck.

"Holy moly!" Andrew shouted down to Judy. "Something weird is coming! It looks like a mini-Stegosaurus!"

As the monster scuttled along the ground, every ant in its path disappeared. Its sticky tongue snapped up ants so quickly that Andrew barely saw it happen.

Thudd pulled himself higher up in Andrew's pocket to get a better look.

*meep* . . . "Thorny devil!" squeaked Thudd. "Shy lizard. Gentle lizard."

"It's sure not gentle with ants," said Andrew.

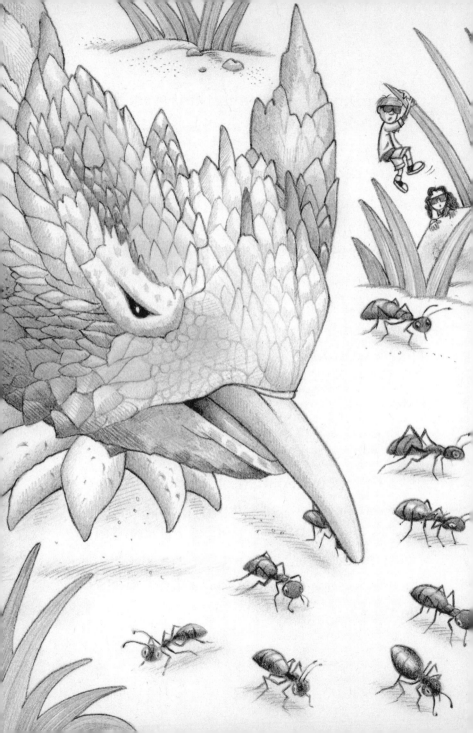

*meep* . . . "Thorny devil gotta eat two thousand ants every day," said Thudd.

Andrew climbed down the stem of grass. "We'd better get our ant-sized selves out of here," he said.

Judy pointed to the pile of rocks nearby. "We can squeeze into a crack between those stones," she said.

As the thorny devil dined, the streams of ants became trickles.

Andrew and Judy sped to the rock pile. They squeezed themselves into a narrow space underneath the stones.

"I think we're safe here," said Andrew.

"And it's cool," said Judy, mopping sweat from her face. Through the crack, they watched the last few frantic ants skitter away.

Swaying back and forth on its dragon-like feet, the thorny devil lumbered past Andrew and Judy's hiding place.

*meep* . . . "Thorny devil move like leaf

blowing along sand," said Thudd. "Can change color to match ground. Camouflage. Hard for predators to see."

"What would want to eat *that* guy?" asked Judy.

*meep* . . . "Big birds. Big lizards, too," said Thudd.

Andrew leaned back against the rock. "Woofers!" he said. "I'm bushed."

In the dimness above, Andrew glimpsed something dangling down. It was long and dark—and wiggling.

*Whew!* thought Andrew. *It's just a little worm. Or maybe a caterpillar. They just eat leaves.*

Judy poked Andrew. She pointed toward the patch of grass they had just left. "Something's moving," she whispered.

Andrew sat up. The blades of grass were shaking. It wasn't the wind.

Suddenly a yellow snaky-looking head

with huge yellow eyes poked out of the grass.

"What's *that*?" whispered Judy.

*meep* . . . "Gecko lizard," said Thudd.

"Another stupid bug-eater!" said Judy. She squeezed herself deeper into the rocky cave.

The gecko was as still as a stone. Its eyes stared unblinkingly in their direction.

*meep* . . . "Drewd and Oody not move," Thudd squeaked softly. "Gecko hunt what move."

Andrew watched the shadow of the worm jiggling just above them.

Suddenly the gecko became a blur. Andrew felt something slam into his stomach. One of the gecko's sharp, hard toes had pinned him against the rock! Andrew looked up to see the gecko snapping at the worm above them.

The next second, a dark triangle appeared above their heads.

*meep* . . . "Death adder snake!" squeaked

Thudd. "Got tail that look like worm! Hide in rocks. Wiggle tail to lure prey animal.

"Death adder got terrible poison. One bite got enough poison to kill eighteen humans."

In a flash, the gecko turned and darted away. The snake's mouth stretched open. From below, Andrew glimpsed its long white fangs. The death adder sprang at the speeding gecko.

Andrew was suddenly soaking wet! Super-smelly stuff was spraying from the rear end of the gecko!

"Eeeeew!" hollered Judy. "Something stinks a hundred times worse than dog poop!"

The death adder slammed its jaws shut on the gecko's tail. The tail broke away like a loose tooth! And it kept on wriggling in the snake's mouth!

*meep* . . . "Gecko spray stinky, stinky stuff at predator," said Thudd. "If predator not let go of tail, gecko let tail go. Grow new tail again."

The tailless gecko raced away and disappeared behind a termite mound.

Andrew held his breath as the last wiggly bit of the gecko's tail slid into the death adder's mouth. *Will we be next?* he wondered.

# SO FUZZY, SO SOFT, SO NOT A KITTEN . . .

The death adder's tongue flicked from its closed mouth.

*meep* . . . "Snake smell stuff with tongue," said Thudd quietly.

The thick yellow-and-brown-striped death adder slithered slowly away from the rock pile. It looped its way over the sand. Andrew and Judy watched it till it was too far away to see.

*meep* . . . "Sun gonna set," said Thudd. He pointed to the sun, now lower in the sky and more orange. "Lotsa animals gonna wake up. Start to hunt. Big danger."

Judy slapped at her clothes, trying to get rid of the sticky, stinky gecko spray. "Yeesh!" she said. "I smell like a litter box!"

*meep* . . . "Nose get used to smell," said Thudd. "In little while, Drewd and Oody not smell stinky stuff anymore."

Andrew shrugged. "Maybe the smell will keep some dangerous animals away," he said.

The sky lit up with ribbons of color—orange and rose and red and purple. Far away, Uluru rock glowed like polished copper.

Judy lifted her sunglasses to get a better look.

"Cheese Louise!" she exclaimed. "Wild colors!"

*meep* . . . "Desert sunset got lotsa color," said Thudd, "cuz desert got lotsa dust.

"Color happen when light bounce off stuff. Light bounce off dust in desert air."

"Let's pick up the pace," said Andrew, trudging ahead. "It'll be dark soon."

Judy rolled her eyes. "It's been hours," she said. "And we're only a few yards from where we started."

"If we could only find a way to use the wind. It's blowing toward Uluru," said Andrew.

"It feels cold," said Judy.

*meep* . . . "Desert air cool fast, fast, fast," said Thudd. "Desert air not got much water. Water in air is what hold heat."

Big, airy tumbleweeds bounced over the sand and grass and sped away.

*Hmmm,* thought Andrew. "Maybe we could . . ."

Just then, he felt the ground shake a little. He looked around.

Behind them were dozens of leaping creatures as tall as refrigerators. They jumped as high as they were tall. Some could have bounded across a classroom in a single leap.

"Wowzers schnauzers!" shouted Andrew. "Kangaroos!"

"A whole *herd* of kangaroos!" said Judy.

Some of the kangaroos stopped to nibble on a bush.

*meep* . . . "Bunch of kangaroos called mob," said Thudd. "Kangaroos looking for grass and leaves to eat."

"The kangaroos are about a billion times bigger than we are," said Judy. "If one of them stomps on us, we're kangaroo toe jam. Let's find somewhere to hide."

Andrew and Judy took off.

*Thumpa! Thumpa! Thumpa!*

They managed to reach a witchetty bush just as the kangaroos were almost on top of them.

Kangaroos were stopping to nibble leaves.

*Chuck, chuck, chuck!* a kangaroo called loudly.

*THUMP!* A kangaroo foot slammed down next to Andrew and Judy. It was so close that a giant black claw brushed the tip of their toes! The next instant, the kangaroo leapt off. Its humongous claw sent them tumbling across the sand like bug-sized golf balls.

Suddenly they stopped rolling and started falling down and down into darkness.

The kangaroo had tossed them into a

hole. But it wasn't just a hole. It was the entrance to a steep underground tunnel.

"Oooof!" hollered Andrew.

"Aaaack!" yelped Judy.

Andrew whammed into something soft, something furry. Downy hairs tickled his neck and legs. *Feels like a kitten,* thought Andrew.

"Where *are* we?" asked Judy.

Andrew whipped off his sunglasses. He unclipped his mini-flashlight from his belt loop and flicked it on.

The beam lit up a cave that was almost filled with a giant, hairy lump the size of a person's fist.

# DEEP TROUBLE

Andrew scratched his head. He couldn't make out what it was. But it wasn't a kitten.

*Eek!* squeaked Thudd. "Whistling spider! Tarantula!"

"Yaaaaaah!" screamed Judy, backing away. "I *hate* spiders even when I'm bigger than they are! And this one's a hundred times bigger than I am! Let's get out of here!"

Andrew put a finger to his lips. "It looks like it's asleep," he said softly. "Don't scream. You'll wake it up."

"Spiders don't have *ears*, Bug-Brain," said Judy. "Where's the way out of the tunnel? It's too dark to see."

*meep* . . . "Spiders hear with hairs on legs," said Thudd. "Smell with leg hairs, too. Can tell if stuff is good to eat."

As Andrew searched for the way out, his beam flickered on a white blob above his head. It looked like a big paper balloon. There was a raggedy hole at the bottom of it.

When his light passed over the hole, Andrew could see small white creatures crawling over each other inside. They looked like eggs with legs.

*meep* . . . "Baby spiders," said Thudd.

*"More spiders!"* said Judy. "Get me *outta* here!"

One of the big spider's dark, hairy legs twitched. Then it stretched. Soon another leg twitched and stretched.

"It's waking up!" screamed Judy.

Andrew's light fell on the opening to the tunnel. Judy raced for it.

As Andrew clambered after Judy, he shoved the back of his flashlight against his forehead. A suction cup at the back made it stick.

*meep* . . . "This spider hunt in nighttime," said Thudd. "Desert too hot in daytime. Make spider dry out.

"If spider lose lotsa water, legs get soft. Like plant that wilt. Then spider legs too soft for spider to walk.

"Getting cool outside. Spider coming out soon, maybe. Gotta hurry!"

Judy found a soft strand of spider silk in the tunnel. They used it to pull themselves along.

*Aroooooo! Ow! Ow! Owooooo!*

Chilling howls drifted into the tunnel.

"Wolves!" said Andrew.

*meep* . . . "Dingoes!" said Thudd. "Wild Australian dogs. Hunt in packs like wolves."

Below the howls, Andrew heard a soft sound.

*Whhhhooooooooo* . . .

*The wind,* Andrew thought.

They were close enough to the top of the tunnel to see that it was nighttime now. The moon was full and bright.

The view outside went dark for a second.

*meep* . . . "Tumbleweed rolling over spider hole," said Thudd. "Tumbleweed break loose, roll across desert, spread seeds long, long way."

"Shhhhh . . . ," said Andrew.

Andrew thought he heard a soft scraping sound at his back. He turned.

His beam reflected off many round, shiny black eyes in a hairy face. The spider was close behind them. It was getting closer every second.

THUDD

# DOUBLE DUBBLE TROUBLE

*Uh-oh,* thought Andrew. His heart was pounding in his ears. *Will we* ever *get out of here alive?*

"Move it, Judy!" he hollered. "The spider's right behind us!"

*"EEEEEYAAAAA!"* hollered Judy. She lost her hold on the strand of spider silk and fell on top of Andrew.

*Eek!* "Go, Oody! Go!" squeaked Thudd. "Spider gonna bite with fangs. Spider juice turn Drewd and Oody insides into goo. Then spider suck out Drewd and Oody goo like milk shake."

Judy got a grip again and scrambled furiously up to the top of the hole. Spider silk covered the edge of the entrance. Andrew and Judy grabbed on to it and pulled themselves out into the cool desert night.

*Sssss . . . sssssss . . . sssssss . . .*

The shadow of a giant claw passed over Andrew's head. He looked up.

In front of them was a lobster-like creature as long as a person's hand. Its fat front claws jabbed the air. Its spiked tail curled over its back.

*"AAAAAAAAACK!"* screamed Judy. "Scorpion!" She tried to run. She fell. Her feet were tangled in the silk that surrounded the edge of the spider burrow. *"HELP!"*

*Eek!* squeaked Thudd. "Scorpion eat anything that move. Eat other spiders. Even eat baby scorpions."

Andrew's knees wobbled.

Judy was screaming and kicking. "Play dead, Judy," said Andrew. "Scorpions eat what moves."

*Hssssssssssssssss* . . . came a sound from behind them—from the spider hole.

*meep* . . . "Whistling spider whistling," said Thudd. "Whistle when it scared."

Andrew shuddered and looked around.

Leg by furry leg, the whistling spider was creeping from its burrow. It reared over them like King Kong.

The scorpion's tail twitched above its head.

*meep* . . . "Scorpion getting ready to sting," said Thudd. "Got poison claw at end of tail!"

The scorpion's claws jabbed at the spider.

"HELLLLLP!" hollered Judy, still caught in the silk. The clawed feet of the spider and the scorpion scraped against her as their battle raged on.

Andrew crept in among the furry legs and the armored legs. He grabbed Judy's hand and tried to pull her up, but a furry leg knocked him away. The spider was pacing quickly back and forth, trying to avoid the scorpion's claws.

Andrew crept behind a pebble and waited for another chance to get Judy.

*Hsssssssssssssssss* . . .

*Sssss . . . sssss . . . sssss* . . .

With its front legs, the whistling spider furiously scraped hairs from its abdomen and tossed them at the scorpion.

*meep* . . . "Spider got poison hairs on abdomen," said Thudd. "If poison hairs land in eyes of scorpion, on soft parts of scorpion, scorpion leave, maybe."

"What if the poison hairs land on Judy?" asked Andrew. "She's right under the spider!"

*meep* . . . "Hurt a lot," said Thudd.

The scorpion clamped a claw on to one of the spider's legs. The spider backed away. The end of the spider's leg snapped off!

*meep* . . . "Spiders got skeleton outside of body," said Thudd. "Called exoskeleton.

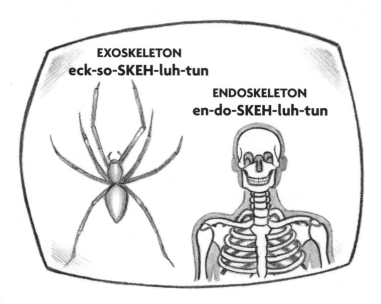

"To grow, spider gotta shed old skeleton. Called molting. When spider grow new skeleton, spider grow new leg."

"Wouldn't it be great if people could do that!" said Andrew.

Andrew caught sight of something racing toward the spider-scorpion battle. It was moving so fast that it was hard to see. But Andrew could tell that it was about the size of a mouse. It leapt onto the scorpion!

The scorpion let go of the whistling spider. The whistling spider turned and scrambled back into its hole.

Judy finally yanked herself free of the spider silk. She raced over to Andrew behind the pebble.

"A mouse attacked the scorpion!" said Andrew.

*meep* . . . "Not mouse," said Thudd. "Animal called fat-tailed dunnart. When dunnart find lotsa food, extra fat get stored in tail.

"Fat-tailed dunnart is marsupial like kangaroo. Tiny babies born small as grain of rice. Crawl into pouch to grow."

"It's *cute*!" said Judy. "And it saved my life. If it hadn't come along, the spider or the scorpion would have stepped on me or eaten me!"

*meep* . . . "Dunnart look cute," said

Thudd. "But dunnart is scary fighter. Attack big prey."

The dunnart had turned the scorpion on its back and pinned it down with its paws. The scorpion was frantically waving its claws. In the shadowy moonlight, Andrew couldn't tell who was winning.

Behind the life-and-death struggle, a huge lump appeared. It was low to the ground and as long as an alligator.

# A BRIGHT IDEA

"What's *that*?" asked Andrew.

*meep* . . . "Big, big lizard," said Thudd. "Called Perentie lizard. Eight feet long. Only bigger lizard is Komodo dragon."

"Uh-oh," said Andrew. "It's sneaking up on the dunnart."

"That brave little guy kept me from getting eaten by a spider," said Judy. "I wish we could save it."

"Hmmmm . . . ," mused Andrew. "Bright lights in your eyes can blind you for a few seconds, especially when your eyes are used to the dark."

Andrew pulled the flashlight off his forehead. As he swept the beam over the ground toward the lizard, light fell on the dunnart and its scorpion prey.

The dunnart looked up for a second—just enough time for the scorpion to escape and scuttle away.

Andrew's beam found the lizard's eye. The lizard stopped in its tracks. Then it turned and lumbered off in the direction it had come from.

The dunnart was still. It was staring at Andrew and Judy. It crouched.

*Eek!* squeaked Thudd. "Dunnart lose scorpion prey! *Drewd and Oody gonna be dunnart prey!*"

"Quick!" said Andrew. "Our only chance is to climb up the witchetty bush. Maybe the dunnart won't be able to follow."

They scurried up into the branches. The dunnart was scrambling up behind them.

In the distance, Andrew could see Uluru glowing golden in the moonlight. The wind whooshed. Tumbleweeds bumped each other as they rolled toward the faraway rock.

"Wowzers schnauzers!" said Andrew. "I know how we can use the wind! We'll get a tumbleweed to take us to Uluru!"

"But the tumbleweeds aren't close enough for us to grab on to," said Judy.

Andrew tugged his ear. "Hmmm . . . ," he murmured.

He turned up the tip of his shirt collar and unzipped a secret pocket underneath. He pulled out something that looked like a short piece of rubber band with a black rubber cup at each end.

It was the Drastic Elastic. It could stretch just about forever, but if Andrew gave it a big jerk, it would snap back instantly.

"I've got the Drastic Elastic," he said. "And I've got an idea. Come on, Judy."

Andrew attached one of the Drastic Elastic suction cups to his flashlight. He crept along to the edge of a witchetty bush twig. He wrapped the Drastic Elastic around himself and around Judy, then he tossed the flashlight at a tumbleweed rolling by.

The flashlight hooked the tumbleweed like a big fish! Andrew jerked the Drastic Elastic. In an instant, Andrew and Judy zoomed through the air! They landed on the prickly tumbleweed.

"Yeeeouch!" hollered Andrew.

"Yiiiiiikes!" hollered Judy.

They pulled themselves off the prickles of the tumbleweed and hung on. The bush rolled along like a beach ball.

"UUUURRRRF!" Andrew burped.

As the tumbleweed rolled, all around them were spooky night sounds—the howls of the dingoes, the clatter of the crickets and katydids, the screams of invisible birds.

*meep* . . . "Purple button blinking!" squeaked Thudd.

# NEEDLE IN A FIELD OF HAYSTACKS

The purple button in the middle of Thudd's chest popped open. A purple beam popped out and at the end of it was a pale purple Uncle Al hologram. His eyebrows came together like fat caterpillars in the middle of his forehead.

"Hi, guys!" he said. "I've been trying to reach you, but I've had trouble with the Hologram Helper."

"Hey, Uncle Al!" said Andrew. "We're in a tumbleweed! We're rolling toward Uluru rock!"

"Good golly, Miss Molly!" said Uncle Al. "You did it! You found a way to use the wind!

"I'm super proud of you guys. Winka and I are at Uluru right now."

"But how are you going to find us?" asked Judy.

"Do you have your flashlight?" asked Uncle Al.

"Yup," said Andrew.

"Turn it on," said Uncle Al.

"But it's such a small light," said Judy. "How can you see it in this huge desert?"

"Winka brought her telescope," said Uncle Al. "It can find the tiniest glimmers of light from stars that are billions of miles away. Now we'll use it to find a speck of light that's much closer."

Andrew reached over to where his flashlight was caught on a tumbleweed twig. He turned it on.

Suddenly the tumbleweed stopped tumbling.

"Uh-oh," said Andrew. "The tumbleweed

must be stuck on something. And we're still pretty far from Uluru rock."

"Look!" said Judy. "Headlights! Is that you, Uncle Al?"

"Probably," said Uncle Al. "There's not much traffic out here. We're going to stop so we can use the telescope."

Andrew and Judy watched the headlights come to a standstill.

"I have an idea," said Andrew.

He untangled his flashlight and the Drastic Elastic from the tumbleweed.

He climbed onto a twig near the outside of the tumbleweed and began to twirl the flashlight like a lasso.

The flashlight made a big circle of light as it went round and round.

"I see you!" said Uncle Al. "Even without the telescope."

Now the headlights began moving toward them. They could see Uncle Al and Winka waving! They were getting out of the jeep! They were running toward the tumbleweed!

Uncle Al picked up the tumbleweed, gently plucked Andrew and Judy out of it, and placed them in the palm of Winka's hand.

"Ooorf . . . ," Judy burped. Her eyes rolled dizzily.

"Blurk . . ." A sound between a hiccup and a burp came out of Andrew.

"Hiya, Unkie! Hiya, Winka!" said Thudd.

"There's a great pizza place at Uluru," said Uncle Al. "They even have witchetty grub topping!"

Even by moonlight, Winka could tell that Andrew and Judy were looking a little green.

Winka smiled kindly. "How about pepperoni?" she said.

"Ooooorp!" said Judy.

"Give me five minutes!" said Andrew.

TO BE CONTINUED IN ANDREW, JUDY, AND THUDD'S
NEXT EXCITING ADVENTURE:

# ANDREW LOST

# WITH THE FROGS!

In stores July 2008

# TRUE STUFF

Thudd wanted to tell you more about delicious witchetty grubs and thorny devils, but he was busy saving Andrew and Judy from meat-eating ants and death adders. Here's what he wanted to say:

• The thorny devil has a big lump on the back of its neck. If a predator attacks this slow-moving lizard, the thorny devil tucks its head between its front legs. The lump on its neck looks like its head! Even if the predator takes a bite of the fake head, the thorny devil has a chance to escape and live.

• Every living thing needs water to survive.

The thorny devil has a way to make sure that it collects every drop that touches it. The thorns of this lizard make little grooves on its skin. All these grooves lead to its mouth. When a thorny devil steps into water or rubs against a dewy plant, the grooves act like straws—they pull water right up to its mouth!

The water is pulled up by what scientists call capillary action. Water molecules in small spaces "climb the walls." For example, if you touch the edge of a paper towel to water, you will see the water spread through the paper. The water is climbing into the tiny spaces between the paper fibers. To see the paper fibers, rip a dry paper towel apart and examine the ripped edge. A magnifying glass will help you see the fibers more clearly.

• It's difficult for animals to survive extreme heat or extreme cold. The molecules we're made of work slowly in the cold. If it gets too cold, they stop working completely. Extreme heat can break the molecules of living things. That's why we cook food. And it's also why very high fevers are dangerous—too much heat can damage the molecules of our brains and other organs.

Interestingly, low fevers actually help our bodies fight infections.

• Many animals keep their eyes clean by blinking. But geckos can't blink—they don't have eyelids. Instead, a transparent scale covers and protects their eyes. When their eye covers get dirty, geckos clean them with their tongues!

• Frogs can survive environments that are too cold or too hot. During cold winters, frogs sink to the bottom of deep lakes. Their hearts slow down and they may even stop breathing. (Frogs can get oxygen through their skin.) Some frogs can freeze almost as solid as an ice cube. They have a kind of "antifreeze" in their blood that keeps their hearts and brains and other organs alive.

Surviving low temperatures by slowing down is called hibernation (hy-bur-NAY-shun).

Desert frogs have the opposite problem, but a similar solution. When the environment becomes too hot and dry, desert frogs burrow underground. It's much cooler down below. They may surround themselves with a layer of shed skin or slime to protect themselves from drying out. Then their bodies slow down, too.

When animals slow down their bodies to deal with heat, it's called estivation (es-tuh-VAY-shun).

• Meat ants are also farmer ants. They protect the caterpillars of certain Australian butter-flies from predators, including other ants. In turn, the caterpillars poop sugary stuff called honeydew—tasty food for ants!

• A brown tumbleweed rolling across a desert is not a dead plant; it's a plant that's spread-ing its seeds.

Tumbleweeds sprout in spring and bloom

in late summer. As soon as the seeds develop, the stem breaks away from the roots. The plant curls into a ball shape and rolls and bounces along the ground. With every bounce, it drops some of its seeds. A tumbleweed can roll for miles, scattering 250,000 seeds along the way.

Tumbleweeds grow well in farmlands. It's easy for the plants to roll and bounce across the open fields. But farmers don't like tumbleweeds. Their sharp thorns can hurt farm animals. Also, they catch fire easily—a burning tumbleweed can destroy a farm.

THUDD

# WHERE TO FIND MORE TRUE STUFF

All deserts are different. But they're all inhabited by plants and animals that have amazing ways to survive with little water and in lots of heat. Want to find out more about desert weirdness? Read these!

• *One Day in the Desert* by Jean Craighead George (New York: HarperTrophy, 1996). A dramatic story of how the humans and animals of the Sonoran Desert in Arizona deal with the heat and a sudden violent storm.

• *Correctamundo! Prickly Pete's Guide to Desert Facts & Cactifracts* by David Lazaroff (Tucson, AZ: Arizona-Sonora Desert Museum Press, 2001).

Do you really know the facts about deserts, or do you just think you know? Find out!

• *101 Questions About Desert Life* by Alice Jablonsky (Howell, UT: Southwest Parks & Monuments Association, 1994). Become an expert on desert facts!

• *Lizards Weird and Wonderful* by Margery Facklam (New York: Little, Brown Books for Young Readers, 2003). Want to know about lizards that squirt blood out of their eyes? Read this book!

Turn the page
for a sneak peek at
Andrew, Judy, and Thudd's
next exciting adventure—

# ANDREW LOST
# WITH THE FROGS

Available July 2008

# GOTTA WEAR YOUR WANNABEE

"Ergh!" grunted ant-sized Andrew Dubble. Andrew, wearing a furry black-and-yellow-striped jumpsuit, was on a ledge outside a kitchen window.

His arms were covered by black metal tubes jointed at the elbows. He was struggling to get his legs into pants made from the same tubes.

"You're not supposed to be outside, Bug-Brain," came a voice from the windowsill behind him. "And what's with that *stupid* outfit?"

It was Andrew's thirteen-year-old cousin, Judy. Judy was ant-sized, too.

Andrew stood up stiffly in his metal pants.

"I figured that since we're bug-sized, we need some bug advantages," he said. "So I made us these suits. They're called Wannabees."

*meep* . . . "Hit Drewd!" came a squeaky voice from a pocket in Andrew's Wannabee.

It was Andrew's little silver robot and pocket-sized best friend, Thudd.

"That's the best idea I've heard since we got shrunk," said Judy. She made a fist and punched Andrew hard in the chest.

"Ooof!" she said, rubbing her hand. "It's hard as a rock!"

Andrew clomped over to a peanut shell on the windowsill. He reached in and pulled out a Wannabee and sets of black tubes like the ones he was wearing. He held them out to Judy.

"This one's for you," he said. "Try it on. I think it's your size."

"You've got to be kidding!" said Judy. "It looks *soooo* uncomfortable. Besides, every one of your stupid inventions has gotten us in trouble. If we just stay in the house, we won't need this junk."

Andrew shook his head. "We can't just hang around the house," he said. "We've got to help Uncle Al save the frogs."

Judy rolled her eyes. "Ever since Uncle Al told us about the disappearing frogs, that's *all* you think about," she said.

"Some frogs have even gone extinct," said Andrew. "Uncle Al needs our help. There's a frog pond just beyond this yard. We've got to go there and see what we can find out."

"Right," said Judy. "At our size, it will take us a year to get to that pond."

"No, it won't," said Andrew.

Andrew reached into a pocket and pulled out a tiny black remote control. He pressed some of its buttons.

Suddenly a dead leaf at the end of the window ledge fluttered. It lifted. Beneath was an odd flying machine. At the top was a pair of large, buggy-looking wings that had been wired together. Beneath the wings were two little seats, and under them were three wheels.

"Cheese Louise!" said Judy. "What is *that*?"

Andrew smiled and cocked his head. "It's the GNAT," he said. "*GNAT* is short for **G**lobal **N**avigation **a**nd **T**ransportation."

"*Global!*" said Judy. "That stupid-looking thing wouldn't get you from here to the kitchen sink."

"You wanna bet?" said Andrew. "I'll bet you the last crumb of Uncle Al's super-delicious fudge. I've got it in my pocket."

"Hmmmm . . . ," Judy pondered. "I'm *sooo* hungry. Okay."

Andrew pressed more buttons on the remote.

*Whrrrrrrrrrrrr* . . .

The GNAT's wings fluttered slowly at first, then faster, then so fast that they seemed to disappear.

Whirring softly, the GNAT lifted a couple

of inches off the windowsill and set itself down in front of Andrew.

Andrew got into the left-hand seat and fastened his seat belt. He patted the seat next to him. Judy climbed in and pulled her seat belt across her shoulder.

He pointed to pedals beneath each seat. "We'll both have to pedal to keep the engine going."

Andrew and Judy started pedaling, but nothing happened.

"I told you so," said Judy. "Give me that fudge crumb."

"Not yet," said Andrew. "The GNAT is storing energy as we pedal. It's like winding up a toy plane."

*WHHHHRRRRRR* . . .

Suddenly the GNAT's wings were beating. The wind from the wings bent Andrew's antennas and blew Judy's hair over her face. The GNAT lurched from side to side, then it zoomed off the window ledge and into the trees.

# Bring magic into your life with these enchanting books!

Magic Tree House® series
by Mary Pope Osborne

The Magic Elements Quartet
by Mallory Loehr
Water Wishes
Earth Magic
Wind Spell
Fire Dreams

Dragons
by Lucille Recht Penner

Fox Eyes
by Mordicai Gerstein

King Arthur's Courage
by Stephanie Spinner

The Magic of Merlin
by Stephanie Spinner

Unicorns
by Lucille Recht Penner